Puss in Boots

❦ Fairy Tale Treasury ❦

Adapted by
Jane Jerrard

Illustrated by
Susan Spellman

Publications International, Ltd.

There once was a poor man with three sons. When the man died, the three divided up their father's belongings. The oldest took his house, the middle son got his mule, and the youngest was left with a cat.

The cat told the youngest son, "Master, give me a sack and a pair of boots, and you'll find yourself the luckiest son of all." Since he had nothing to lose, the young man did as the cat asked.

The cat put on the boots and took the sack to a place where he knew many fat rabbits came to find dinner. Soon enough, Puss caught a plump rabbit in his sack.

He carried his catch straight to the castle of the King! Puss bowed low and offered the King the rabbit. He said, "Sire, please accept this gift from my master, the Duke of Carabas." (For that is the name he had chosen for his master.)

A few days later, the cat returned and gave the King a pair of fat white doves, and a few days after that, he brought a dozen quail eggs.

For several weeks, Puss brought gifts to the King. Each time, he explained that the presents were from the Duke of Carabas. The king was charmed by such a well-mannered cat, and enjoyed the presents very much.

One day after visiting the king, Puss came to his master and told him to take off his shirt and breeches and stand in the river near the bridge at noon. His master did as he was asked. Soon the King's carriage crossed the bridge, and Puss cried out, "Help! My master, the Duke of Carabas, is drowning!"

The King knew the cat, and the name of the Duke. He ordered his guards to save the man.

Puss told the King that his master's clothes had been stolen, so the King sent for an extra suit of his own clothes. The Duke looked quite handsome in the fine clothes. The King's daughter, who was riding in the carriage, told him so.

The King invited the Duke to ride with them. The cat ran ahead of the royal coach, quite pleased with himself.

As he ran ahead of the coach, Puss ordered every farmer and worker he met on the road, "You must tell the King that the land you work on belongs to the Duke of Carabas. If you do not, the Ogre who lives in that far castle will chop you into tiny pieces for stew!"

When the King stopped to ask whose land he crossed, he heard, "The Duke of Carabas!" no matter how far he went.

"You certainly have a lot of land," the King said to the Duke. The Princess smiled at him, and the new Duke smiled back, thinking how beautiful the princess was.

At last Puss came to the great castle, which really did belong to an ogre—and so did all the lands they had passed through. Puss knew all about the Ogre. He went into the castle and asked to see him.

"I hear that you can take the shape of any animal you choose," said Puss to the Ogre. "I hear you can, if you wish, become a lion."

The Ogre said that this was true, and he turned himself into a lion. Puss waited until the Ogre turned back into his own shape.

"People also say that you can change yourself into a mouse," said Puss, "but that is impossible!"

The Ogre changed himself into a mouse right then and there. Well, Puss gobbled him up in one bite! Just then, the King's carriage arrived. Puss ran to meet it, saying "Welcome to Carabas Castle."

At the cat's orders, the Ogre's servants gave the guests a wonderful meal. It was decided that the Princess and the Duke of Carabas should marry. As for Puss, he never had to hunt for mice again—except sometimes for fun!